We
Have
A Baby

Cathryn Falwell

Clarion Books • New York

Clarion Books
a Houghton Mifflin Company imprint
215 Park Avenue South, New York, NY 10003
Text and illustrations copyright © 1993 by Cathryn Falwell

For information about permission to reproduce selections
from this book, write to trade.permissions@hmhco.com or to Permissions,
Houghton Mifflin Harcourt Publishing Company, 3 Park Avenue, 19th Floor,
New York, New York 10016.

Printed in China

Library of Congress Cataloging-in-Publication Data

Falwell, Cathryn.
We have a baby / Cathryn Falwell.
p.   cm.
Summary: The arrival of a new baby is a cause for celebration,
presenting opportunities to love, watch, touch, and care for
the new family member.
ISBN 0-395-62038-4   PA ISBN 0-395-73970-5
[1. Babies—Fiction.] I. Title.
PZ7.F198We 1993
[E]—dc20
94-40268   CIP   AC
LEO   30 29 28 27 26 25 24 23
4500710308

For Max
and his family

We have
a baby!

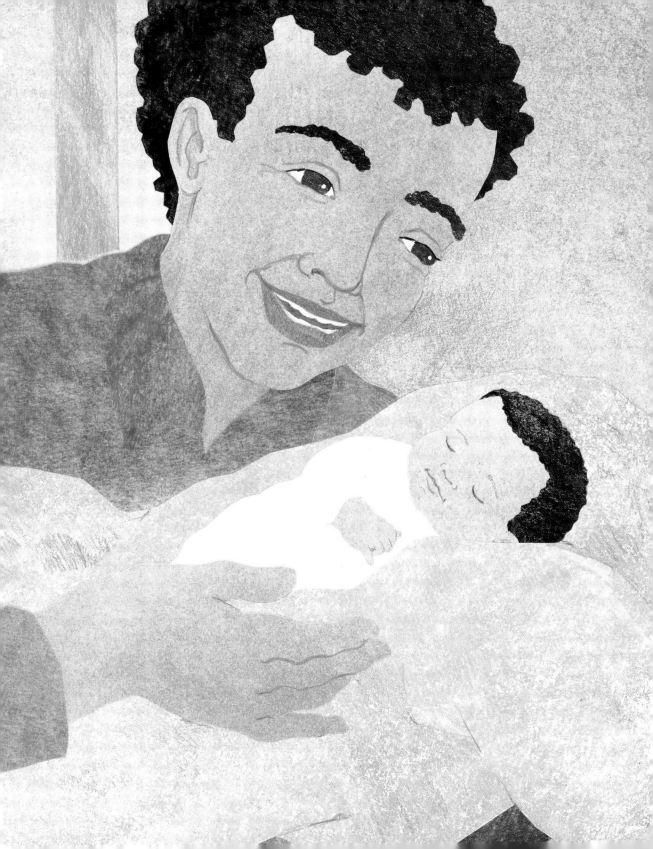

A baby
to love

A baby
to watch

A baby
to touch

A baby
to take
care of

A baby
to wash

A baby
to dress

A baby
to feed

A baby
to carry

A baby to hold

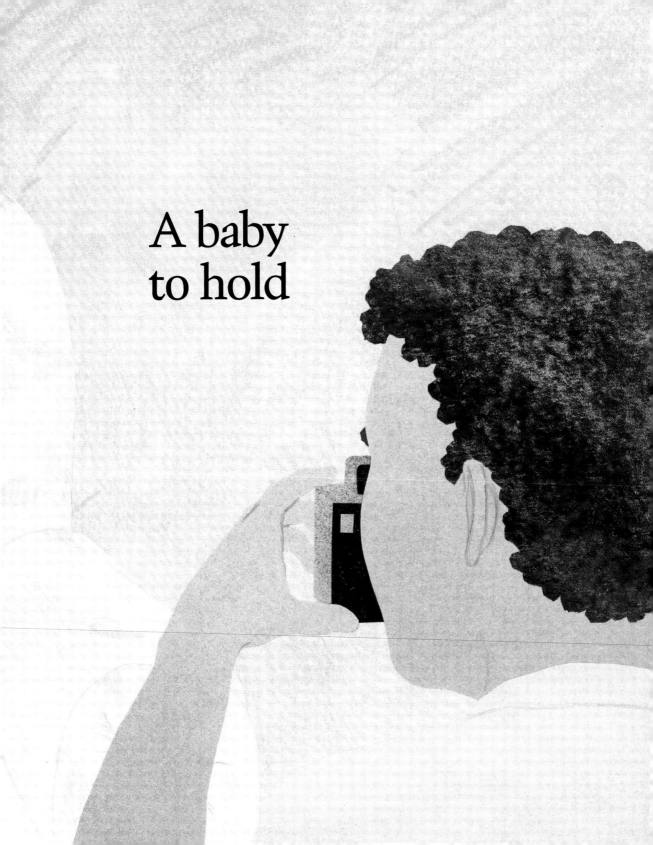

A baby
to kiss

A baby
to rock

A baby
to love

A baby who loves us.